HAN M GREENBARG

Elf Bat Book Two: Sacrifice

First published by starlighteineadhpress 2021

First edition

ISBN: 978-1-73-250296-3

This book was professionally typeset on Reedsy.
Find out more at reedsy.com

Shadow Cold
Life Forgotten
Awoken Suffer
Dreams of Flame And Ruin
Brethren of Honor

Ne'er Disloyal
Surrender To Love
Defend
Family
Warriors

—The Elf Bats of Sidhovvn And The Breath
Of Their Creator,
Han M Greenbarg

Contents

1

Vinhdiragh

SPINDLE

The cascading snake of stars hung low above the outer villages, crafting a pulsating glow over each white rooftop. Ialchagor's Cliff shadowed over the night, ten Elf Bats perched on its weathered edge. Spindle stood silent beneath them with his crew in the thick of the forest, awaiting Kiah's word to charge forth across the open meadow. He sensed the stir of rage in the Bats and felt their desire for a great scourge upon the purebreds of Sidhovvn.

The eight villages were positioned around the perimeter of Adreachterum like a scattered flock of white birds. Each housed specific artisans and their brood who answered to King Averee and his ruthless Bloodmanghe. The dark of the night weighed heavier than it ever had before. It had been years since Spindle had set foot among the purebreds, years since he turned his back on the people who had scarred everyone he loved. The beauty of the purebred Elves went no further than their physical appearance. The intentions of their hearts and minds were full of malice.

Vinhdiragh, Spindle thought. *This is the signal to run. This is the signal to avenge their blood. Defend the outcasts until our end. Defend the broken hearts to our death.*

He looked up at the sky. Vulkie and Fire had created a fog with their wings on the cliff's edge. The stars were no longer visible.

"Vinhdiragh!" Kiah shrieked from the top of Ialchagor. His brethren echoed him in the cry.

"Yes," Spindle whispered. His fingers grazed the hilt of his sword as he readied himself to sprint. *Dive, Bat.* He heard the steady breath of his crew behind him, each of them heavily armored and wielding brutal weapons. Spindle knew that Elf Bats were prone to intense emotion. There was little hope that their presence would go unnoticed in the night. Little chance of a stealth mission. *Allegiance to the Elf Bats*, Spindle thought. *This is for you, Kiah.* He closed his eyes, feeling the wind tousle his earrings into the tangled dark hair at his shoulders. *For your people.*

FLY

Fly looked down the line at her Bat brethren as they leaned forward to drop into a synchronized dive off the cliff. She felt their rage. Their hearts were filled with the spirit of Vinhdiragh. Vengeful, bitter, desiring a violent justice. Then she looked at Kiah, his eyes fixed on the city before them. He held a different sort of power in his body. It was, as Spindle had explained to her, the potent mixture of Vinhdiragh and Ilumiaoacht, in which a Bat's physical and mental strength surged to the greatest level of power one could bear.

Fly stood with them, prepared to defend what she love. She bore the spirit of Ilumiaoacht in her heart— her fight was out of love alone, not anger. She felt their pain and ached for them, but she had yet to know the feeling of Vinhdiragh within herself.

Kiah did not look at her, and Fly wondered for a brief moment if he sensed their child within her.

KIAH

Stay close to me, my love. Trust your training.

"I trust it," Fly said aloud. "I'm with you until whatever end."

The strength in her voice filled Kiah with pride. He shrieked once more into the night, dropping off the edge of the cliff, wings pressed tight against his body. Fly and the Bat brethren followed, diving in formation. They opened their wings four inches from the ground, whirling back into the sky and dispersing across the city.

Kiah and Fly flew to the top of the citadel, perching themselves side by side. He looked at Fly as she stared at something beneath them.

What is it?

The windows. The walls. Everything has been rebuilt. All glass. This is vain foolishness of the king.

And that concerns us?

Fly smirked as she thought, *To our advantage, beloved. Easier to destroy.*

Kiah nodded and in a harsh whisper said, "Averee knows not of our revenge."

None of them feel it, Fly agreed.

We wait for the signal, Kiah thought. *Then we go to Count Addis.* He scanned the darkness, eyes unable to make out any movement beneath them. *Promise you won't do anything rash.*

Without looking at him, Fly wrapped her claws around his. *I can't promise that.*

Why not?

I'm married to you, Hezekiah. You're my king, I'm your queen. We are both reckless.

"Aye," Kiah whispered. "That we are."

What if the others get into trouble? Fly thought.

Then we have their back, pudding.

Fly half-smiled up at Kiah. *I got your back too.*

2

Gracious War

TSUNAMI

Tsunami dropped quick and silent from the sky, crouching low on a patch of damp soil. He contained his breathing behind closed fangs and a tight throat as he crept through the dirt. *Once descended*, Tsunami thought, *do not return to the air until Kiah's call for home.*

Raihatiac, the furthest village from Adreachterum, was a haven for artisans of jewelry and stained glass, where any young purebred Elf could grow from apprentice to master in the family's shop. Count Llieghonu was the head of Raihatiac, and from what Tsunami remembered before being blinded, Llieghonu had silver in the tips of his brown hair and beard, priding himself on appearing more human than Elf. Tsunami hadn't been certain that he was, in fact, a purebred count of the king, but Llieghonu proved it during his malicious acts of torture on Banegildacht. Only a purebred Elf knew how to inflict the most agony on a Bat.

Memories of Autmhae, Father, and Mama overwhelmed Tsunami as he stood and walked forward, cautious of each motion he made in the sleeping village. He knew the direction of Llieghonu's home because of the strengthening cherry blossom scent. He had never smelt anything like it before Banegildacht.

He touched the door frame with the tips of his claws, feeling the rotting, splintering wood. It was not a new structure, yet there was a space surrounding him that felt open to the moonlight. He ran his claws across the left of the frame, faltering at the smooth glass. The frame was old, the glass new. Rough edges, yet a pristine guile. Just like Llieghonu.

Twelve Years Earlier: Banegildacht

"Let your sister sleep, Soo. This is not the time to practice your storytelling."

Nine-year-old Tsunami stood by the cradle, looking up at Mama with wide eyes. "But I have to tell someone! The white dragon won't make it through the mountain passage if I don't show him the shadow on the wall."

Mama chuckled. "And what is the name of this white dragon?"

"I think he wants to be called Stormwind."

"Well," Mama said, "tell Stormwind to wait until he's in his room before he starts roaring. Autmhae needs her rest so her wings can grow."

"I'll go tell Father."

"Not while he's reciting the ancient text."

"But Mama, I have to tell this story!"

"Shh. Quiet, Tsunami."

Tsunami blew a loud sigh, slumping his shoulders. The tips of his wings grazed the cave floor as he turned around. "Okay, I'll wait for you and Father in my room."

"We'll come say goodnight. I promise."

"And listen to my story?"

"Aye," she said with a gentle smile. "And listen to your story. Go on, young one."

The sounds of the sea outside the cave soothed Tsunami as he returned to his room. Their home was one of the few carved out within the Ocedhaim Cliffs, the waves ever crashing and rolling, the salt in the air a healing element to the Bats fortunate enough to live in such a rugged and tranquil landscape.

He was a master at entertaining himself, preferring to stay up way past midnight and sometimes crawl into his baby sister's room after Mama and Father had gone to bed, just so he could share his latest tale with the aid of shadow puppets. Autmhae didn't yet laugh or talk back, but she was a good listener.

"Where was I?" Tsunami asked the dark. He approached the torch burning near his bed and knelt under it. "The dragon had come to stir up the commoners. All he wanted was an adventure. Every dragon sought trouble in the city, and Stormwind was no different." He opened his wings, admiring the shadow they made on the wall. Only an Elf Bat could act out a dragon so naturally. Wings were a gift. "He flew above the city, diving into the narrow passageway." Tsunami rose up and spun in a circle, spreading his arms to the ceiling. He spoke loudly as he continued his story. "The dragons joined together in chaos. The commoners screamed."

At his last word, a shriek sounded from deep within the cave. A horrific sound Tsunami had never heard before.

"The baby! Vikariillen, the baby!"

Mama was calling out to Father in a high-pitched voice.

"Save Autmhae! Get her out! Vikarii! Vika—"

Her words were cut off.

"Soo, get out of the cave!"

Father. Tsunami ran out of his room to the nursery where Autmhae slept in her cradle.

"Save your sister!" Father screamed. He sounded hoarse and far away.

Tsunami had no understanding that death had arrived for his family, but his young Bat body suddenly felt the agony of his father and the loss of his mama. *Someone bad has come,* he thought. He picked Autmhae up, clutching her against his chest.

"Bring me the son. Bring Tsunami."

The voice of the invader.

"Take the female's body outside and burn it."

More voices. Echoing all over the cave.

"It's not real. It's just a dream. We're waking up soon. It's okay, Autmhae." He whispered into her ear. "I'll tell you another story."

"You! C'mere, Bat!"

No. Tsunami met the eye of a giant soldier and ran toward the back of the cave. The edge of rock that dropped into a great chasm with a flow of dark water at the bottom. He had never calculated the distance from ledge to landing, but he thought if he could protect Autmhae from the impact, they would float back up and escape farther into the tunnel that led to the ocean.

"Tsunami, son of Vikariillen. Aren't you the spitting image of your father? Such unique features for a Bat. Fair face, gold hair, no trace of filth on your clothes." The invader spoke with an eloquent grace as he stepped close. "The legendary Bat eyes. Multicolored irises."

Tsunami responded, keeping Autmhae tight in his arms as she started to cry. "Father says me and Autmhae are regal. We're scholars." He bounced in place, anxious as the giant soldiers came next to the invader.

"Give me the baby."

"I can't. I have to keep my sister safe."

"Think you can jump? Think you can fly? Your wings are young, boy."

Tsunami looked down at the drop. "I'm not scared."

"The baby."

"No. You can't have my sister." He opened his wings and leaned back.

"Take him now!"

Tsunami felt himself yanked forward as the soldiers surrounded him and pried baby Autmhae out of his arms. He gasped for breath when one of them gripped him by the throat and held him over the ledge.

"Let's kill the Bat here, Llieghonu."

"We take him to see his father, Grail. Come. You can have the baby Bat."

Grail threw Tsunami hard onto the cave floor and followed two other soldiers back through the corridor. Tsunami looked up into the face of the invader who was now grinning down at him.

"Bring the boy to his father."

Before he could utter a protest, Tsunami saw another soldier stand over him and lower the butt of an ax with tremendous speed. The young Bat lost consciousness.

It's a dream. Where are we going? Mama, where are you? Where's Autmhae? Baby sister, I'm here.

Tusnami opened his eyes to see that everything was upside down. He struggled to breathe in the grip of a soldier, then gasped as his body was dropped to the cold stone floor of his parent's room.

"I've done nothing to you or your people," Father was saying to the invader. "I've done you no evil."

"Vikariillen, by order of the king, you must be sacrificed."

"Not in front of my son. Please. Please, make him go."

"Averee has made it clear that no Elf Bat should live to see the future of Sidhovvn or Adreachterum. I, Count Llieghonu, must see to his bidding."

"Father?" Tsunami looked around the room, making eye contact with each soldier and the invader who called himself Llieghonu. He pressed a hand to his forehead, wincing at the pain. "Father?"

"Soo, go."

Father was laying on his back, chained to the bed. His eyes were glassy with tears.

"Father..." Tsunami hesitantly approached. He saw the blood and breathed heavy as he realized what was happening. It was not a dream.

"Soo, please. Go."

Tsunami backed away, only to bump against another soldier who gripped his shoulders, restraining him as he watched the terrible scene continue. Father's wings were ripped out, his body sliced with swords, his rib cage stabbed over and over as he shrieked and writhed in agony.

"Little Tsunami. Son of Vikariillen." Count Llieghonu knelt in front of the young Bat.

"Where's Autmhae?" Tsunami asked, tears streaming down his face. "Where is she?"

Llieghonu held up a single cherry blossom in front of his face. "My wife planted these for good luck in our garden. You could use luck, little Bat. You've lost everything." He stared from the blossom to Tsunami, who was sobbing and trembling in the hold of a soldier. "Remember this sight." He walked away, letting the blossom slip through his fingers.

"Where's Autmhae? Where's Autmhae?" Tsunami screamed, fighting against the soldier who shoved him down on his back.

"Do it," Llieghonu ordered from outside the room.

"Let go of me! Let go!"

The giant soldiers took the lit torches that were placed around the walls and threw them directly into Tsunami's eyes as he was beaten into the ground. An hour later, he saw nothing but darkness and heard nothing but his own weary breath.

Present Day: Vinhdiragh

"If not for the claws, fangs, and wings, you could fit in with my people. Oceanic eyes. Angelic gold hair."

"Llieghonu," Tsunami growled. He lowered himself to the floor, shifting his weight as delicately as a spider about to jump from one thread to the next.

"Why are you here in my house? I have no fight left. No reason to be attacked."

"Autmhae," Tsunami whispered. "She was so small."

"A Bat child means nothing to the king."

"Mama and Father."

"All sins must be forgiven, Bat. Even by the most unworthy creatures in Sidhovvn."

"Everything you did to my father that night, I'm going to do to you. Every last torment." Tsunami crept forward, rising from the primal animal crawl into his straight-shouldered, eight-foot march. Count Llieghonu backed down the hallway, feeling for any weapons hung along the wall.

"Your wife is out," Tsunami said. "Your children are sleeping elsewhere. It's just us."

"You won't finish the job like I did." Llieghonu's eyes remained cold as Tsunami pulled the blades from behind his wings and crossed them in front of his chest. "I should've killed you then, Bat."

"Aye." Tsunami grinned as he heard the count hastily grab a spear from the floor. "You should have." His face changed from mirth to ferocity as he charged forward, shoving the count through the glass window.

Blades in hand, Tsunami stepped through the shards of glass and out onto the roof. Llieghonu grunted as he rolled to his side, hands scrambling for the spear he had grasped. Tsunami sensed the rising fear in him, the vulnerable state of his body and mind.

"Tell me," Tsunami hissed, "what happened to Autmhae?"

"The baby Bat never opened her wings." Llieghonu stood up. Tsunami held his blades out as he circled back, finding the edge of the roof. "We watched her fall."

"You dropped her from the edge."

"Yes."

Tsunami whirled forward, spinning into Llieghonu, striking his blades against the spear. "It's your turn to be sacrificed, Llieghonu," he spat. "You wear no armor. No cloak. My pirate allies will soon have your Bloodmanghe occupied."

"You know this much about me, Bat? You're blind. I took your sight to make you weak."

"Then allow me to make it an even fight."

Tsunami attacked with relentless energy, surprised at Llieghonu's defense as he warded off each blow. But where the count's stamina was waning, the Bat only grew more vicious with every swing of his blades. Finally, he heard the count drop to his knees.

"Act on your anger, Bat," Llieghonu said, "and I swear you will regret it forever."

Tsunami's arm shook as he raised his left blade.

"The Elf Bats are creatures of the dark, and my blood will forever be on your hands. Do not be as wicked as your beloved king Kiah."

There is none more wicked than you, Llieghonu, Tsunami said in his mind. *I will regret nothing in this life except failing to save my sister.*

"I am no creature of the dark," he spat at Llieghonu. "You are." He heard a defeated sigh in the count's chest and snarled as he drove the blade through his heart. "For Autmhae."

3

Wretched Wind

HURRICANE

Hurricane motioned for Spindle's crewmen to stay behind as he cautiously entered the house of Count Iratsuad. Six torches lined the wall to his right, the soft orange glow lighting up the room and highlighting the rug on the floor. He stepped on it and shuddered. Not a rug. It was an old skin and wings of an Elf Bat. Leathery, cold, a prized possession of the count.

For you, Mama. Without pity. Hurricane closed his eyes and touched his claw against his chest. *Payment is due.*

"Evening, Bat." The count stood in the middle of the hallway, a candle in one hand. He calmly gestured to Hurricane's missing limbs, nodding as if he had been expecting the midnight visit. "You should have bled out that night."

"The goblins saved me."

"Outcasts helping outcasts. Fitting."

Hurricane took out his left blade, staring down the count who remained stoic. "You tortured my family to death. Mama, Father, all six of my siblings."

Iratsuad said nothing, moving slow as he kept his eyes on Hurricane.

He glanced toward the rooms of his children and a look of concern crossed his face.

"Fight me," Hurricane said.

"I'm all my children have, Bat. Their mother is gone."

"You forced my siblings to watch you torture Mama. How can I leave you alive?"

Iratsuad noticed the taunting gleam in the Bat's eyes. He backed away. "Where are my children?"

"Fight me."

"Where have you put them?"

Hurricane followed the count as he grew more panicked, moving further down the hallway in his search for his young son and daughters. "Fight me, you coward. Fight me!"

"Tell me now!" Iratsuad turned, raising the candle between them. "What have you done?"

Hurricane whispered the names of his family as he circled the count. "Calenduihla, Artheadiv..."

"Tell me, Bat! Where are my children?"

"Clovaidh, Elwaias, Anhgra..."

"You tell me right now."

"Elaisah, Sailhna, Iliianrai."

"Or I will sever the arteries in your throat."

Hurricane watched him drop the candle and grab a scimitar from the wall behind him. "You have my word, Iratsuad. I will look after your children better than you ever did."

"I don't want to give in to violence, Bat."

"But you want to see me dead. Fight me."

Iratsuad took a swing and Hurricane met the blade with his own.

Twelve Years Earlier: Banegildacht

Hurricane ducked as a crust of bread came flying toward his face.

"Enough, Clovaidh. If you must throw food at your brother, do it outside."

"Is Father coming home soon?"

"Not for a while. He's busy painting."

"Why does he stay so late in the forest? He can paint here."

"Because," Anhgra said, trying to sound authoritative, "Mama doesn't like the mess inside the cave. Same reason we can't have a food fight or play mud tag in here."

Red-haired Elaisah stood up on her chair. "I love mud tag!"

"Mind your voice at the table, love. You're spitting all over."

"I can't help it, Mama. My fangs are loose."

Hurricane looked around the table at his siblings. His four younger sisters were the loudest in way of shrieks and chatter, but it was his big brother Clovaidh who made the largest messes and had his back in every squabble.

"Caine, as you are second born, you have the honor of being demoted to three fewer pillows in the shredding contest."

"Being the eldest does not make you the commander, Clovaidh. I'm going to cheat as always."

"How is that fair? Mama, is that fair?"

"I leave the debate to you, child. I do not know your pillow shredding rules." She chuckled as she looked at her sons.

Iliianrai, the youngest, dribbled orange berry juice all over the table as she bounced in her seat. "When do I get to play?"

"When your fangs are fully set in your head." Clovaidh traded eye rolls with Hurricane and their brother Elwaias. They never finished a pillow shredding match without one of the girls crawling in and demanding to join a team. "Iliia, you don't want us to knock them out, do you?"

"I can bite the pillows. Anhgra said I'm the princess of the cave and I get to do what I want."

"Boys, go on to your room. Angrah, you can help me clear the table tonight."

"Mama, I don't want to help. It's not my turn."

"Aye, you said that last night too, didn't you? Come. It's near bedtime."

Caine giggled with his brothers as their sister delved into a list of reasons why she shouldn't have to do her chores. They made for the hallway, eager to start their pillow shredding, but a purebred Elf appeared out of nowhere, blocking their path.

"Where is Artheadiv?"

The purebred was decorated in thick armor, looking sternly down at the young Bats. "Where is Artheadiv?" he asked a second time. His eyes shifted to Mama. "The Bat wife. Calenduihla."

Hurricane noticed Mama silently corral the girls under the table before she spoke to the purebred stranger. "Who are you?"

"Count Iratsuad. Where is your husband?"

"In the forest."

"Tis a shame to hear that. He's going to miss the horrors within this cave."

"Why are you here? Do you not come from the city?"

"I'm the head of Iragaodh. I was sent by the king."

"Why?"

"The sacrifice. You, your husband, your children." Suddenly Count Iratsuad lunged forward and grabbed her by her hair, pulling her toward the floor. Mama lashed out at him, spitting into his face and pushing him away. The count refused to back down. He forced himself on top of her as she shrieked and flailed.

"Let the children go," she said, her voice trembling. "Don't let them see this."

"Worry not, Calenduihla, it will only be a moment."

Unable to take more of Mama's cries and the sight of his little sisters cowering under the table, Hurricane ran up behind the count and struck his back with his small claws. "Leave my mama alone!"

"Ibex!" the count yelled out, still perched on top of Mama, who was struggling to breathe under the weight of his armor.

A soldier as tall as the ceiling came into the room, pushing past Hurricane and Clovaidh with one sweep of the arm. He whirled to face them.

"Bloodmanghe," Hurricane heard his big brother whisper. He had never seen Clovaidh so frightened. Nothing should've scared him. But this Bloodmanghe soldier did.

"Ibex," Count Iratsuad said from his position on Mama, "take my place."

Hurricane watched both of his brothers back toward the table and quietly duck under it, putting their arms around their sisters in a protective embrace. He stayed out in the open, standing under the threatening gaze of the intruders.

"How old are you, boy?" Iratsuad approached Hurricane as the soldier went to Mama's side. "Seven? Nine?"

"I am Hurricane, son of Artheadiv. I am ten years old, and I will fight you." He tried not to let his voice waver even as he held back tears.

Iratsuad laughed. "Fight? When your body is as brittle as a leaf at autumn's end?"

"My father is coming home. He will drive you out."

"Your father is already dead."

Hurricane glowered at the count, feeling a tear slide down his face. "I will fight you, Count Iratsuad."

Four more Bloodmanghe appeared, surrounding his brothers and sisters, forcing them all out from under the table and into the furthest corner with Mama. Ibex bent and slid one of his swords toward Hurricane, gesturing for him to pick it up.

"Show us then, little Bat," Iratsuad said, "that you can fight."

Hurricane had never wielded a metal weapon. Never held one. He reached for it, grasping the hilt and growling as he struggled to lift it. He stared up at where the blade ended far above his head.

"That's a two-handed sword," Iratsuad said, clearly amused at the sight.

"He does not have the arm strength," Ibex the Bloodmanghe said with a bellowing cackle.

"Fight me!" Hurricane screamed. His voice echoed in the cave. "Fight me!"

Father had said an Elf Bat never attacks without being provoked. One should only lift a blade with the intention to defend...never to kill. He glanced toward Mama, his brothers and sisters, helplessly huddled together and surrounded by soldiers. He would do whatever it took to defend them.

The count nodded and Ibex came forward swinging his blade. It was a light attack at first, mocking, almost playful with the young Bat. Hurricane bared his fangs, desperately trying to look ferocious, as he had seen his father do in their games of Bat tag in the forest. His arms trembled as he kept hold of the blade, finally making contact with the soldier's chest armor. It was thick, heavy, impossible to damage.

Within minutes of the weak-spirited duel, the count uttered the words: "Ibex, finish him."

Present Day: Vinhdiragh

"The Bloodmanghe took my arm and leg off so fast. I don't remember anything after that until I was revived by the goblins. That's when I saw what you had done."

Iratsuad grinned maliciously under the light of a bedroom torch. "The Elf Bats are going to be wiped out one way or the other, Hurricane. My children will avenge my death."

"Then I will raise them myself. I will teach them the sins you committed."

"Tell me where they are."

"Nothing more shall be said about your progeny, Iratsuad. You owe me." Hurricane drove his left blade into Iratsuad's rib cage and violently thrusted it upward. The scimitar slipped from the count's hand as he dropped to his knees and looked up into the Bat's eyes. "Never provoke an Elf Bat, count. Your life is mine."

The count's body hit the ground.

"Vinhdiragh," Hurricane whispered. "Tonight, we are wild." He backed away from the corpse and sprinted to the well that was dug thirty feet from the house. The dead count's children huddled together at the bottom, sheltered from the dark elements that were about to collide around them. Looking over the edge, down at their frightened faces, Hurricane could only see his own brothers and sisters peering back at him. His throat clenched as he turned away. "I will come back, children. Stay silent as the shadows."

4

Flower Light

<u>*SNOWBLIND*</u>

I do this for you, Adreinnha. You and our daughters. Snowblind stepped across the threshold, breathing softly. To his right was a dark hallway, no torches illuminating the floor or walls. Hardly any light in the house except for fading embers in a hearth. No sign of Eadmeihn.

"Master?" said a small voice. Snowblind looked down. A child looked back at him. A little girl. He slowly lowered himself to one knee. "Are you a daughter of Eadmeihn?"

She stared at his claws then back at his eyes. She started to back away.

"It's okay," Snowblind said gently. "It's okay."

"Elf Bat," a quivering voice said behind the girl. The wife of Eadmeihn.

Snowblind looked to his right and his left. "Where is your husband?"

"He's not here."

"No? Tell me where."

The woman held up her hands, tears streaming down her face. "Please, Bat, leave us be."

"Where is Eadmeihn?" He moved forward as she clutched her daughter to her chest and warily stepped back toward the hearth. Two older girls were ducking down behind a chair.

"I had three daughters too, my dear," Snowblind said. "Near the same ages as yours."

The woman looked horrified as she pushed her youngest child behind her.

"Tell me where he is."

"Don't harm my children."

"Your children are safe. I will not hurt you or your daughters." Snowblind took off his cloak and knelt by the hearth. He stoked the embers with the tips of his claws. "Your husband needs to pay for what he did to my family."

"They need their father, Bat. It matters not what happened. Your kind are wretched."

"Are we? And what makes us so?" He turned his back to them and took off a layer of armor along with half of his blue bodysuit, showing the constellation of tattoos on his shoulder. "Do you see this? The lotus flower is for my beloved Adreinnha. She was my wife, the only woman I will ever love. The pinecone is for Ehnadha, my eldest daughter. She was an adventurer and loved poetry just like me and her mama. The daffodil is for Inekiana. Our middle girl with the most contagious giggle." Snowblind made eye contact with Eadmeihn's smallest daughter as she hid behind her mother. "And the orchid," he said, pulling the tunic back over his head and fastening the clasp of his cloak, "is for Meaghiea. My youngest. She should not have died that night. She should not have been violated by Eadmeihn."

"He didn't torture the Bat children," the woman protested. "He wouldn't!"

"I am here for one purpose. Take your daughters and leave the house."

"No."

"You don't want to see what happens next, my dear."

He whirled at the sound of creaking stairs and cocked his head when he saw there were none.

"I am astounded," came a raspy voice from above. "You've come right on time."

Snowblind drew in a sharp breath. "Where are you, count?"

A hidden stairway opened from the dark hallway and Count Eadmeihn calmly stepped down, several books under his arm. "I'm sure you would love to explore my library, Bat. I remember burning all the books in your cave."

"Were you warned of our coming?"

"A few villages are more prepared than others, but there is no set of weapons in my home. Not since I chose to make it a safe haven for my daughters."

Snowblind snarled at Eadmeihn's mocking grin. "You violated mine."

"How would you know? Weren't they already dead when you found them?"

"My wife was alive."

"Yes, she was a spirited Bat female. Your little girls were enchanting too."

"Don't speak of them."

Eadmeihn dropped the books he was carrying and motioned for his wife to remain in the room. "Why did you come so late to the massacre?"

"I had to bury my grandparents...they were killed by someone else."

"The humans, right? No one likes you, Elf Bat. No one likes your kind."

Snowblind stared down into Eadmeihn's eyes. *You have no right to be the leader of Floseadrom.* "My wife was alive. She was alive. I could've saved her."

<u>*Twelve Years Earlier: Banegildacht*</u>

The Torchaien river ran parallel to the human city Herradhtadya, just north of its gate. Snowblind pushed the last of the soft dirt up against the second tombstone and whispered a final goodbye to his grandparents. He stood, running the tips of his claws down his white tunic, and glanced up at the night sky. *Midnight. Time to go home to my beloveds.*

Flying was not safe near the human city, so Snowblind was forced to start a brisk walk toward home. He leapt across the river and made his way silently in the direction of the southernmost forest. A scream stopped him in his tracks. It was not a scream he had ever heard before. *Adreinnha.* She did not sound angry or fearful. She sounded like she was in pain. Agony. "Adreinnha!"

Snowblind ran, wings unfurling behind him as he came through the thick trees. More screams. Smaller voices. Fragile, delicate cries. *Meaghiea.* Branches crashed around him as he noticed the soldiers of the king galloping on horseback alongside him, their terrifying faces glowering as they veered off in a different direction. Smoke and flame crackled in the distance. Shrieks of Elf Bats weighed on Snowblind's heart as he stumbled into the clearing surrounding the entrance of his cave.

Bat blood and wing fragments covered the ground. One small body was hung upside down on a tree limb. For a moment, Snowblind hoped he had found life, and hesitantly reached out to touch the chest of the hanging Bat body. The heartbeat was gone.

"Meaghiea." He gripped what was left of her wispy red hair, drew her lifeless face into his chest and wept. "My little Meaghiea."

Snow...

Snowblind looked around the clearing, fighting to hold back a wail.

My Snow...

Suddenly he saw Adreinnha in the carnage. He let go of his youngest daughter's body and knelt beside his wife. She was alive.

"Adreinnha, my love."

"They attacked us," she said, her voice pained.

"Who did this?"

"Count Eadmeihn violated the girls." Adreinnha spoke with a shudder. "Snow, I listened to their cries. They cried for me and I could do nothing."

She wept in Snowblind's arms as he cradled her.

"My love," he whispered. "I should've been here."

She shook her head. "Your grandparents were loved too."

"I should've been here."

"I get to see you now," Adreinnha said. She stared up into his eyes, her body trembling. "You'll be all right, Snowblind."

"Adreinnha, I'm taking you into the cave. We have medicine. I can heal your wounds."

"No," she said in a hoarse whisper. "Too much blood is already lost. Go somewhere safe."

"I can't. Adreinnha, I'll get the medicine. It's in the library."

"Go, love," she said.

Snowblind stood, lifting her body with him. "Come on. We'll fix this. I'll help you." He felt Adreinnha take one more breath as he held her limp body in his arms. Her spirit and her voice were no longer with him. She was gone. A guttural cry tore through his body, filling him with rage.

"Eadmeihn," he screamed in madness, "it's your turn! Your turn to die!"

Present Day: Vinhdiragh

"Eadmeihn, it's your turn."

"My turn?" The smug count chuckled, looking around at his family. "You would stab my heart out in front of my children?"

"There is no mercy left for you." Before the count could open his mouth to respond, Snowblind drew his blades and ran them into Eadmeihn, pushing him all the way back down the hallway as he heard his wife and daughters scream. "No time to forgive what you have done."

Eadmeihn tried to breathe in, tried in desperation to grasp one of the blades lodged in his lungs as Snowblind forced it deeper into his body and snarled at the sound of cracking ribs and bone. "You did the bidding of your king, Eadmeihn, so I do the bidding of mine."

Bright red blood spewed from the count's mouth as he surrendered to the execution. Snowblind drew his blades out and closed his eyes at the sight of Eadmeihn's lifeless body slumping to the floor. Crimson stained the tips of his blades as he listened to the family's sobbing behind him. He stared at the blood and whispered, "Adreinnha, you are avenged."

Stepping back out into the night, he lifted his head to the stars. He gave a sigh, closing his eyes as the wind rustled his long white hair. *The horn of Adreachterum. News has reached the king.* The deep, melodious hum of the artisanal instrument traveled through the villages faster than he had ever heard it. *So it begins.* At the sight of movement to his left, Snowblind opened his wings and took off toward the city with as much speed as he could gather. *The Bloodmanghe are coming.*

SPINDLE

Everyone can hear that horn. Spindle spun in the direction of the citadel, earrings jingling in the tangle of his matted hair. He had positioned the majority of his crew around Adreachterum's perimeter, and within seconds of the horn blowing he heard the clash of blades as the Bloodmanghe popped out of their hiding places to defend their territory. *Stealth is no longer an option.*

Spindle scrambled to a rooftop and looked for the Bats who had returned from their acts of vengeance. The darkness was suddenly punctured by small spouts of flame. The Bloodmanghe were lighting up the sky to catch anything that moved within it. *Tsunami. Snowblind. Hurricane.* He recognized each Bat by their flight pattern, and in the midst of a brewing battle between seven hundred hulking Bloodmanghe and his own meager lanky warriors, Spindle knew the bloodshed had just begun.

"C'mon, Kiah," he whispered. "Take down the king and fly home."

KIAH

Something's wrong. At the top of the citadel, Kiah looked at Fly and slowly rose to peer into the darkness. *The Bloodmanghe.*

They answer to the horn, Kiah. We knew they would be drawn out.

Not this fast. Kiah felt a shiver in his wings. *It can't be this fast.*

5

Winter's Eve

TORNADO

Twelve Years Earlier: Banegildacht

Father is dead. Tornado couldn't stop crying as he hid behind Mama.

"Bring me the female." The purebred count half grinned, seeming to be amused by Mama's feisty spirit. "Separate the young ones."

"Bloodmanghe," Mama spat at the soldiers. "I do not fear you."

"You think your kind is beautiful? That you are worthy of respect?"

"Leave my children alone, demon."

"You will call me Count Fiieguin," he said. His fist flew, landing a punch across her mouth.

Mama shook her head like a rabid dog, flinging her dark hair about as she lunged at the count. "Purebred snake," she shrieked.

"Your sons will watch you die, she-bat, before we decapitate them."

One of the Bloodmanghe came behind Mama and forced her onto her knees. She looked at her boys who were held at the point of a broadsword, each of them looking back at her in fear. *It's okay. It will be okay*, she said to them in her mind as the count circled her with a predator's gaze.

What will we do without Father? Tornado's eldest brother Crystaithn thought.

Mama... Tornado found himself staring up at Count Fiieguin. "Why did you kill my father?"

"You boys have a lot to learn," the count said. "I'm about to show you one of the real world consequences of being an animal."

"We're not animals, count," Crystaithn said with a quivering voice. "Can you let Mama go?"

Fiieguin spoke to the Bloodmanghe while facing the young Bats. "Bind the female and hold her down." He turned around. "Keep the children back."

Tornado watched the count position himself on top of Mama in a manner that only Father had done. He saw the painful defeat in Mama's eyes, realizing that what the count was doing to her was dishonorable. He felt her agony and tears streamed down his face as he looked away.

"Get off her!" Crystaithn and Adeinf charged forward, teaming up to pull Fiieguin away from her, but they were outmatched by the hulking Bloodmanghe.

What did we do wrong? Why is this happening to my family? Tornado's vision blurred as he witnessed the executions of Mama and his three brothers. *Is it my turn to feel the Bloodmanghe's sword?* Nothing made sense. Nothing seemed real.

Tornado sprinted forward, preparing to be grabbed by the soldiers, but he moved past them without resistance. He continued to run through the cave, finding himself in a narrow tunnel. *Other Bats. The Bloodmanghe can't get to the higher caves.* There were other places to hide. *Typhoon. I'll find my best friend,* he thought. *We'll wait this out together.*

Present Day: Vinhdiragh

The horn of Adreachterum had reached the village of Geisperadh faster than he had anticipated. Tornado held his position, blades drawn, as he approached the doorway of Count Fiieguin's house.

"Ambush, Tor! Get out!" The pirates sounded far away as Tornado looked up, to the left, to the right.

"They're coming! We're overrun! Get out, Bat!"

Tornado ran into the middle of the house, blades held at his sides, and in a spontaneous decision charged toward the stairs, meeting Fiieguin halfway up the steps.

"Elf Bat," Fiieguin hissed. "You've made this easy for me."

"Vinhdiragh!" Tornado yelled. He swung his blades, the count swiftly blocking them with the butt of an ax. He lost his balance and barely caught himself on the step beneath him, opening his wings to regain control of his body.

"Take him," Fiieguin mouthed.

Suddenly Tornado was bashed over the head with an empty tankard and wrestled to the ground by a Bloodmanghe.

"I'd stay still, Bat." Fiieguin picked up Tornado's twin blades and grinned as he tossed one of them to the Bloodmanghe.

FLY

Tor, Fly thought. *He's in trouble.*

Kiah nodded. *Be swift and silent, my love.*

TORNADO

"Your mother was a fighter. A lovely, but cruel-mouthed fighter."

"Mama fought for her life," Tornado said.

"She refused my compassion, Bat."

"You showed us none!"

"Ardahk," Fiieguin calmly said to the Bloodmanghe, "take his wings."

No. Not my wings. Tornado shrieked in agony as the burly soldier used the twin blades taken from him to cut into the core of his wings and rip them from his body.

"Cry like your mother," Fiieguin sneered. "Make me feel your pain."

"No...she didn't fear you," Tornado uttered through raspy breaths.

"You fear me, don't you? You didn't plan on being stripped of your wings, but now they're gone. You have no dignity in death." Fiieguin lifted his head with one of the blades. "You will die a common animal. A creature of the lowest scum. Just like your mother."

Tornado wanted to snarl back at him but couldn't. He shuddered at the cruelty in the count's face. The same face that broke his spirit on the night of Banegildacht.

"All Elf Bats are easily broken, and you, Tornado, are one of the broken ones." Count Fiieguin nodded at Ardahk and turned his back, indicating that the Bloodmanghe should dissect Tornado where he lay.

"Siobahorkeilde!" Fly dropped in through the ceiling swinging her blades in rapid synchronization, and with one aggressive downward cut, decapitated Ardahk the Bloodmanghe.

Tornado grinned weakly. *My queen has come.*

How bad? Fly asked.

Wings are gone. Tornado accepted her claw to pull him up. "But he's still mine."

Fly gave a fierce look to Fiieguin before flying back through the gaping hole.

"Well," Fiieguin said, glancing up, "magnificent girl. But she will die the same as you."

"You took my wings from my back, count." Tornado gripped the blades that Fly had returned to him and crossed them at his chest. "I take your head from your shoulders."

The count's shoulders drooped as he breathed out. "Even in my death, you will never escape your demons."

"Don't be certain," Tornado said.

"I am." Fiieguin tilted his head to stare into the colorful Bat irises. "You Elf Bats are cursed."

We are free. Siobahorkeilde. Tor shrieked the war cry as he thrust his blades into Fiieguin's throat. Blood covered his cloak and armor and splattered across the walls. He breathed heavy, thinking back to when he saw Mama pinned under the count's hostile body, her eyes drained of honor. "My queen," he whispered and looked up to where Fly had returned to the sky. "You've returned honor to our women." *Duty to the brethren. Defend until death. Butterfly, you are proving your worth to us all.*

6

Born In Ashes

VULKIE

You don't always get to choose survival. Sometimes survival is a gift. I was given that gift. Da, Mama, Ashnai, and Loerif were not. Why am I alive if not to avenge my parents and brothers? Why else am I following my king and queen into a trap?

Vulkie strode silently past the stable, pausing briefly to pet one of the horses who curiously eyed him. He noted the soft glow coming from within the farmhouse at the edge of the village's perimeter and moved toward it. He saw Count Adheatim in his mind, a fuzzy image from the night of Banegildacht. Barely remembering what was said by the count, but fully embracing the haunting of Mama's spirit. Her singing in his head always woke him from sleep. Ialchagor. The lullaby every Bat grew up with.

Twelve Years Earlier: Banegildacht

Vulkie watched from his treetop perch as Bats chased each other around in the midnight sky. He could only practice climbing trees with his baby claws, and the thought of waiting three more years to fly with everyone was frustrating. *Why can't my wings work now?* he thought. He looked over his shoulder while opening his wings. They were delicate, unable to carry him anywhere.

"I'll be a tree climber. I have claws," he said to himself with a grin.

"Vulkie! Vulkie, where are you?"

Mama's looking for me.

"Vulkie, time to go home! Come, little one!"

All right, Mama. I'm coming. Vulkie sighed. He faced the northeast coast and smelled the salty sea air mixed with lush tree leaves. His favorite smell in the world.

Little one, come down to me, Mama said.

Taking in one last breath of the chilled air, little Vulkie made his way to the branch below him. He paused and turned his face to the west. *Smoke. Hot smoke.* Suddenly a hot, dry wind rushed through the forest. Smoke and flame descended, veiling the stars. He remained frozen, watching in confusion as the tips of trees around him turned into giant candle wicks. The smoke clouded his line of sight and he breathed it in, coughing.

*Vulkie...Vulkie, my baby...*Mama called to him from the ground. Asked where he was. She sounded frightened.

"The forest is on fire! Fly away, Emraidha!" Da's voice was below. "I'll find Vulkie. You go, Emrai! Go!"

Vulkie continued to climb down, all sense of direction ruined. He coughed, swiveling his head to see how close he was to the ground. The ground was nowhere. He was still high in the trees. *I can't get down.* The crackling of the flames within the branches hurt his ears and he wrapped his wings around himself to block the noise.

"Vulkie!" Mama shrieked.

Swords against tree trunks sounded far below him. The shrieks of Bats echoed in the smoke. Vulkie kept coughing. He tried again to find his way back down.

"Leave the bodies, Takled. Let them burn. We have runaways to catch."

Whose voice is that?

"Following you, Adheatim."

Vulkie's feet found the ground and he stumbled forward through the raining embers. Mama's cloak was there. Mama wasn't.

Vulkie...

Mama, where are you?

Stay alive, little one. Stay alive for me.

Vulkie only then noticed the flames enveloping his body. His wings were spared from burns, but the searing pain was everywhere else. Fire lit up his hair and arms as he ran through the forest, blinded by falling leaves and ash and shrieking in agony. He could hear Mama singing in his head. Ialchagor.

Ioah Aei Lirevh,

Aihmdi Doagh,

Araced Aei...

He dropped, breathing in with what lung strength he had left, and closed his eyes. *I'll wake up. I'll wake up soon. This is a dream, Mama.*

Present Day: Vinhdiragh

Vulkie looked around at the lit torches that filled the count's bedroom. *Perfect place to deploy a hail of pyro-cannon,* he thought. Count Adheatim and his wife were in the midst of lovemaking in their bed, and much to the amusement of Vulkie, they did not seem startled by his entrance.

"How are you laying with your maiden, Adheatim? There is chaos all around you."

The count kissed his wife once more before turning his attention to the Bat. "Your kin's chaos cannot interrupt everything." He sat up and casually reached for the shirt draped across the headboard. "But if I must participate in the senseless fray..."

Vulkie made eye contact with the woman. "Leave this house, love. I'm not here to cause you harm."

She hesitated before pulling the bed sheet around her but exited the room without a backward glance.

Vulkie kept his blades sheathed at his back as he watched the count get dressed. "I was four years old that night. The Spitxz saved and raised me."

"You were just a baby Bat. How did you survive the fire?"

Vulkie gestured to his scars when Adheatim looked at him. "Not without a reminder of my suffering."

Adheatim scoffed. "Now you truly look like a monster. Fitting."

You dare name me the monster. Vulkie bared his fangs.

"Just an animal on his last hour before slaughter," the count said. "Come. See yourself in the mirror, wretched beast."

Vulkie tipped his head back, looking up at the ceiling. *Come on, Kiah. Where are you?*

"What are you staring at, Bat?" Adheatim asked. "Hoping for an army to aid you?" He lifted one of the torches off the wall. "You will burn again."

Our trap is set. Now, Kiah!

Vulkie looked back at the count just as the roof of the farmhouse caved in around them. Kiah appeared above the gaping hole, pyro-cannon clutched in his claws.

Light us up, Vulkie said.

Aye, brother. Have your revenge.

Vulkie ran hard, wings unfurled, into Count Adheatim just as Kiah dropped the pyro-cannon. The farmhouse exploded into flames.

"Demon rat!" Adheatim cried. Vulkie gripped his throat, forcing him to lay in the fire. *Payback, count. Face what I endured.*

"Let me up. Let me up, spawn of Spitxz!"

Vulkie's arms trembled with the effort of holding Adheatim down. He drew back, taking out one of his twin blades, and struck the count across the face.

"You'll burn with me, Bat!" the count screamed. He picked up a splintered bit of wood and tried to stab Vulkie, but his own hands were compromised by the fire.

"I am burning with you," Vulkie said. He looked down, seeing his legs engulfed in flames. The heat tightened around his leather armor as he stood firm. "But I do not fear this." He stabbed repeatedly with one blade, arms shaking as the count finally took his last breath. "I'm alive, Adheatim. And I'm staying that way."

7

Fire Snow

FIRESTORM

Twelve Years Earlier: Banegildacht

"My wings are wilted, Fire. I'm heading home."

"It's only thirty minutes past midnight. Drink some of Sprint's father's coffee. It'll keep you awake."

Elf Bat children were packed in the cave's front living room, the drummers and fiddlers in the midst of a raucous revelry. It was a cold night, but the body heat of all the Bats provided warmth. Young Firestorm whipped and bobbed his head, proud to show off the tiny, elegant braids that Mama had worked so hard to weave into his hair.

"I've never heard a better rhythm than this one. The drummers are carrying it well."

"They are," Firestorm agreed.

"But I really am tired, Fire. If I use my wings any longer I'll be hitting the ceiling and tumbling right into those cute girls over there."

"I hear you, Felcore. That would be embarrassing."

"Tell Sprint he throws the best birthday parties. I'll see you tomorrow."

Firestorm and Felcore traded their secret Bat wing-shake and parted ways, Firestorm moving further into the crowd of raucous dancers. From a very young age Elf Bats rapidly developed strong balance and coordination, and the lot of them enjoying Sprint's party knew how to dance.

"Fast as flame, Fire. Just like your name."

Firestorm responded to his schoolmate Esriina as he moved rhythmically with the drumbeat. "Dancing runs in my family. Of course I'm fast."

Esriina traded coy grins with her friend. "I can't wait to see your skill when you are full-fledged, Firestorm."

"Don't think I'll be asking you to dance, Esriina. Your bouncy movements don't work with the intensity of the drums."

The volume of the music rattled tiny pebbles on the cave floor and those dancing closest to the instruments were immersed in a unified trance, unable to break away from the wave of youthful Bat energy. Firestorm lost track of time and place as he did at every dance party, failing to notice the gradual slowing of music around him. He opened his wings, preparing to wildly leap onto one of the hollow drums, when he felt himself shoved to the floor.

"Adnard!" He raised his fist, punching the chest of his friend. "Adnard, what are you—" He choked on his words, eyes widening in horror. Adnard was dead. Two thick arrows pierced straight through his body. A clamor began to grow around Firestorm as he looked frantically around the cave.

"Kill all of them! Leave no Bat child alive!"

Firestorm dropped, flattening himself next to his dead friend. *The music. The drums have stopped. Shrieking. Bat cries.* He noticed the other bodies around him. Decapitated. Wing-less. They had been felled minutes ago. All children. *Why? Who has done this?*

"Ignitehd," said a terribly deep voice. "What of the young she-bats?"

"Do it here."

Get home. Get home, Fire, Firestorm told himself. He lay low, silent as a shadow amidst the growing pile of the dead. He began to crawl, wings dragging on the floor. The cave's entrance was blocked by three massive purebred soldiers. He pressed himself flat and held his breath.

"Averee would love to see these corpses. We should bring some back to him."

"No. Let their legacy rot here. Horrible, disgusting caves. Animal filth will turn to dust in a century."

Firestorm tried to ignore the cruel voices of the soldiers. Their insults hurt his heart. *Why can't I hear your voice, Mama? Are you okay?* He inched forward, breathing out in relief when he saw the soldiers clear out. *Home.* He crawled until he got to the edge of the cave and flew fast and high. *I feel nothing. I hear nothing. My family is gone.*

Present Day: Vinhdiragh

Firestorm touched the door of Count Ignitehd's home and glanced up at the lit torches. He beckoned with his claws to the two pirates provided by Spindle as back-up protection.

"Shadow me," he said. He tested the door, and seeing it was locked, jumped up and unfurled his wings to splinter it to pieces.

At the loud crash, Ignitehd came down the stairs with his wife behind him. With one bleary but vicious look to Firestorm and the pirates, he whirled to face his wife. "Go to the roof."

Firestorm raised a claw as he stared down Ignitehd. "None of you purebreds can explain why you hate us."

"You don't deserve to live."

"Because we don't look like you?"

"Monsters of the underworld do not belong in Sidhovvn."

"You are the monster, count," Firestorm said.

Ignitehd suddenly let out a yell and his wife appeared at the top of the stairs with a smoldering object in hand. She threw it at Firestorm's face right as he ducked. The object exploded against the wall, knocking the pirates and Firestorm to the floor. He coughed in the swirl of thick smoke, the braids in his long hair falling across his eyes as he saw the count reach down to grab him.

"Die, ugly creature."

Firestorm swiftly rolled to the right, feeling for his blades in the dirt. Ignitehed stood over him, driving the tip of a jagged tooth spear into the Bat's back, cracking it through the leather armor against his spine.

Don't take my dancing, Firestorm thought. His pained shriek brought Bloodmanghe out of the shadows. *Not my wings. Not my legs.* His arms were convulsing. "Finish it, count," he whispered.

"Cahlfurodhei!" screamed a Bat voice from the sky. "Cahlfurodhei Eagrottas, Ignitehd!"

Caine flew headfirst into the count, opening his wings to body slam the Bloodmanghe that circled them. "Fire, get up. Come, brother, up!"

Firestorm dug his claws into the dirt and pushed himself to his knees. He grinned in relief when he found he could still stand. He took one step forward and dropped.

"If I can still fight with one arm and one leg, Fire, you can still dance. Use your wings."

Wings of power. Wings of rhythm. Firestorm ignored the pain in his back and picked up his blades. Caine kept the Bloodmanghe distracted while Ignitehd turned again on Firestorm.

"Not paralyzed yet, Bat, but I'll break the rest of your spine."

Firestorm ducked, swinging his blades to block the spear. "For my friends, Ignitehd. May their souls glide with peace in the wake of your execution." He used the angry force of his lithe body to snap the count's spear in half and drove his blades up through Ignitehd's ribs.

Vinhdiragh. Caine stood beside him as they watched the count drop. *Vinhdiragh, my Bat brother.*

8

For K'adhlenalde

KIAH

You dragged Mama's body across the cold, hard ground. Kiah and Fly stood at arm's length from Fractal, the Bloodmanghe who had dealt the final blow to Mama and Father. Count Addis was no longer the priority.

"Go inside, Fly," Kiah told her, blades gripped firm at his sides as he waited for Fly to enter the house.

"K'adhlenalde," Fractal hissed. "My favorite kill."

"Ialkmairde," Kiah spat at him. *Ialkmairde, Bloodmanghe. An insult for a dishonorable soul.*

"K'adhlenalde," Fractal said again. "She was a strong she-bat."

"Don't speak her name!"

Fractal snarled, eyes scanning Kiah for a weakness.

"I found my father's body after you took Mama from me."

"Elf Bats are not worthy of life."

"Why did you hang him upside down?"

"He was an animal. A sacrifice."

"He was a king! I am Jekkiliah's heir, Bloodmanghe, and I take my family's honor back."

Twelve Years Earlier: Banegildacht

"It's time for sleep, little prince. You've worn yourself out."

Kiah bounced up and down on his bed. "I'm not tired, Mama. When do I get to stay up past midnight?"

"You must rest your growing wings. Next year you take your first flight."

"The courage dive?" Kiah said with wide eyes.

"Aye," Father said, joining Mama in the room. "The courage dive."

"But, Father, I'm wide awake."

"Well then," Mama said, "I will sing Ialchagor."

"That doesn't work." Kiah folded his arms as he laid back on his pillow. "I'm not tired."

"Come now," Father said, sitting on the edge of his son's bed. "You do this every night, Hezekiah. And every night we manage to sing you to sleep."

Kiah tried to change the subject. "What if my wings don't work? I could fall and get hurt."

"If the wind fails to catch you, Kiah," Mama said gently, "then your father will. I promise."

"Okay, Mama. You can sing Ialchagor now."

His parents laughed at his resolve, and they both sat with him, trading a loving gaze with each other before they began to sing. As Kiah's eyes started to close, he hummed the last words with them. He was warm. He was safe. Dreams took him, and he slept soundly until the nightmare came.

Present Day: Vinhdiragh

Wings and speed. Vault and spin. Kiah used the entirety of his body to duel Fractal the Bloodmanghe. He spun, blades out, until he was facing the opposite direction. He felt the stale breath of Fractal behind him. The edge of an ax inches above his neck.

"Ioah Aei Lirevh," Kiah chanted in a hoarse voice. "Aihmdi Doagh, Araced Aei." He ducked, whipping his blades against Fractal's armor. "Nefiia Rahh, Aosnn Aei."

"Your mother," Fractal said with a cackle. "The count and I took turns with her."

Kiah let out an enraged scream, driving his blades into the Bloodmanghe's throat, crushing his windpipe, pinning him against the wall. "You die the killer," he whispered. "I live the warrior. Mama's honor is returned."

FLY

Fly stood between Addis and the doorway. She saw the empty wine bottles scattered on the floor, the drunken stance of her father as he stared back.

"You have wings," he said. "You chose life with them. A she-bat."

"I defend them."

"You have taken K'adhlenalde's place as queen, haven't you?"

Fly felt herself tremble in anger. She shook her head as Addis staggered forward. "Don't say her name. You stole her honor."

"You, daughter, are bound to die like the rest of them. In torture and in darkness."

"You will not torture my husband, Count Addis," Fly said. She forced herself to refuse seeing him as the person who had raised her. "He will torture you."

Addis shifted his eyes to Kiah, who entered the house covered in blood. "And you. The Elf Bat who saved Butterfly. You wouldn't kill me in front of her. You don't have the heart."

"You violated my mama."

Addis stepped back, feet failing to move in a straight line. He caught himself on the dining table and placed his hand around a half-empty wine glass. "You will not torture me, boy."

"You dissected bodies. The bodies of my kin."

Fly kept to one corner of the room, terror and pride for her husband swirling inside her head. Kiah's voice was strong, calculating, not a quiver on his lips as he spoke to Addis.

"Do you know, Kiah, I begged Kadhle to return my affection. She would've been spared had she loved me back." Addis brought the glass to his mouth and sipped.

"That's a lie. You basked in her death. I saw your face. I saw you watch her bleed out." Kiah grabbed the drunk purebred by the throat and held him against the table. "You smiled."

Fly noticed Addis trying to grab at another wine glass as Kiah held him in a choke hold. He didn't seem to care whether he lived or died.

"Kiah," Fly said as she approached them. "Addis knew we would come back. Why else would he put himself in this foolish state of mind?"

"You desecrated my people. You dishonored my parents!" Kiah growled at the count's blithe demeanor.

*Kiah...I have to tell you...*Fly started to think aloud, wanting to end the night of violence with the news of the child she carried. But with one chilling look from Kiah, she backed away and lowered her head. *I respect your action,* she thought. *Please, make it quick.*

With one swift motion, Kiah stabbed his left blade into the count's right arm, pinning him to the table, and slashed his knee with the other blade. As Addis crumpled, howling in pain, Kiah glanced back at Fly, seeing the confusion in her eyes. "Allow him suffering that he will carry forever." He lifted his left blade, freeing the count's arm. "Stay inside, count, or I really will kill you."

Now we go to Averee?

Aye, Kiah said. *We confront him together. Come.*

9

Spider in Leaves

<u>*TYPHOON*</u>

Typhoon's Bat instincts reverberated through his wings as he approached the village of Illarandu. Count Uvleorm's house was dark save for one lit torch illuminating a dining room table. He walked past the dining area, glancing down at the remnants of a meal still scattered across the table, and stopped at the window that faced the city of Adreachterum. Spindle and his crew were engaging the Bloodmanghe in a vicious fray. Amidst the sounds of battle echoing around the house, Typhoon kept his head on a swivel, prepared for any sudden attack by Uvleorm.

As a child he had preferred his bow, but Father and his uncles told him to rely on his own body's agility and weight as a force against any outside threat. He prided himself on the muscle he had gained through years of solo training. It was still not enough to barrel through an army of Bloodmanghe, but he could hold his own in a one-on-one duel.

I'll surprise the count, Typhoon thought, as he crouched down and crawled under the table. He remained under the table as he reached one arm up to grab a coffee mug and breathe in what was left at the bottom. Only a few drops left, but it smelled strong and bitter. The same sort of black coffee that he had tasted for the first time on Banegildacht.

Twelve Years Earlier: Banegildacht

"Ty, come sit with your uncles," Father said. "They've got something to show you."

"What is it, Father?"

"You know all those nights you've begged me to allow you some coffee? Tonight's the night, lad. You get to drink it with us."

"Mama, is he being serious?" Typhoon asked with a pout. He watched Mama gracefully arrange a tower of fruit and carry the platter to the dinner table with help from Auntie Ennaeoa.

"Your father isn't teasing you, child. Come. You've been studying in your room far too long."

Typhoon decided to keep it to himself that he had been neglecting his studies, instead spending his hours alone practicing archery. Being the only child of his parents and the sole young Bat in his extended family, he didn't want to make it known that he preferred target practice over Father's wrestling games.

"I get to drink this?" he asked as he sat himself between Uncle Treius and Uncle Agrattin. He pointed at the tankard in front of him, head tilted in awe of the smell wafting from its rim.

"Aye, boy. Go on," Uncle Treius said. He gripped his own tankard of coffee, sipping it with a grin.

Typhoon looked around the table at his family before joining in. The tankard covered his face as he clutched it with both claws and drank.

"See?" Uncle Agrattin said. "I told your parents you would like it."

The table was silent as Typhoon set the coffee back down, everyone waiting for his word of approval. But the moment was interrupted by loud Bat minds.

Hear that?

Outside.

Mama and Father were looking at each other in a strange way. All at once his aunties and uncles rose to their feet, cloaks swirling around them as they rushed to the front of the cave. Uncle Treius came running back and pointed at Typhoon. "Hide him. Hide him, Arranveh," he said to Father. "We'll hold them off."

Father pulled Typhoon out of his chair and sprinted down the hall, wings nearly lifting them off the ground.

"Father, are we playing hide and seek with Uncle Treius again? He never finds me."

"Quiet, Ty. This is not play."

"But I want more coffee."

"Listen, lad, you have to stay here." Father opened the weapons closet, directing Typhoon to get down on the floor. He picked two light swords out for himself and covered his son with a thick blanket. "I have to go."

"Father, wait!" Typhoon pushed the blanket off. "Can't I come?"

"Bloodmanghe have come to our home. Do you not hear the blades?"

"I can fight with you."

"No. Stay, Typhoon. I will come back for you." Father hurriedly closed and locked the door and Typhoon heard him run back toward the dining room.

"Father!" Typhoon cried out. He banged on the door.

"Find their son," bellowed a voice from down the hall.

Father...Typhoon dropped to his stomach and pulled the blanket over himself. A crossbow and broadsword fell on top of him as he belly-crawled further back.

"Leave the bodies," the same bellowing voice said.

"Uvleorm, the king asked us to bring them back."

"He asked me to decimate the lot of them. Let's go, soldier. Fiieguin calls for us."

"What of Arranveh's son?"

"He'll come out of hiding. Watch for him."

Typhoon remained flat on the closet floor and shuddered as the voices passed him by. He waited in the dark surrounded by old iron and pieces of armor, hoping for Father or Mama to unlock the door. They never came.

Present Day: Vinhdiragh

"Cowardly Bat." Count Uvleorm entered the house looking like he had already seen battle, clothes covered in blood. He had his bow drawn and aimed at Typhoon's head. "Not Bat blood if that's what you're thinking. Just the half-breed pirates who keep getting in the way."

Still keeping an eye on Uvleorm, Typhoon reached up from under the table and grabbed a shallow bowl of stew. He brought it to his lips, loudly slurping. It was cold and congealed. *You didn't just kill my family, count.* "Their bloody body parts were strewn all over the cave as if a wild beast has grabbed hold and shook them in their teeth."

"I'm thorough."

They stared each other down, the count's hand steady as he held back the arrow.

"Wife make this?" Typhoon asked of the stew.

"My daughter," Uvleorm growled.

"Not terrible," Typhoon said as he placed the empty bowl on the floor. "But it's no Elf Bat cooking."

With an aggravated roar, Uvleorm aggressively kicked the table leg and it collapsed on top of Typhoon. He fired the arrow into the pile of broken dishes and wood. "Your father hid you from me, didn't he? I sent the soldiers back to look everywhere in that cave and they didn't find the son of—" He paused when he heard terrified screams of his own people outside the house. "Your kind is a plague!" As Uvleorm readied another arrow, Typhoon noticed Tor silently enter through the doorway behind the count's back.

"Go on, count," Typhoon said. He stretched out his arms and opened his wings. "End it."

Uvleorm's fingers twitched in the second he released the arrow. Typhoon spun, blocking the shot with his wings.

"Think I don't know your game, Bat?" Uvleorm said. "Your wings give you an advantage, but I can still crush your neck." He let his bow clatter to the floor. "Hit me, dragon eyes."

Blades, Typhoon thought as he looked past the count at Tor. *Together.*

Uvleorm turned his head to see the second Bat behind him and scowled. He took a swing at Tor with his fist.

"Vinhdiragh," Typhoon and Tor cried together as they stabbed their blades into the count, firmly holding them against his rib cage as he bled out.

Our vengeance, they thought as they watched his lifeless body hit the floor.

"Let's go," Tor said. "The city is overrun with Bloodmanghe."

"Tor...your wings." Typhoon touched his shoulder and saw him flinch. "They took your wings."

"Aye. I'm still alive."

"How did you get here so fast?"

"I've always been a master at sprinting over rooftops. You should remember that after our growing up together."

"I knew you were a champion of tunnel sprinting," Typhoon said. "I won't forget it now, brother."

Tor looked toward the walls of Adreachterum. The rim torches were bright, eliminating the protection of the dark sky. He climbed up onto the roof and hurriedly started for the city with Typhoon flying alongside him. *It's about time we give Spindle proper aid.*

10

Weave Forward

AVALANCHE

Twelve Years Earlier: Banegildacht

"Tag, Beryl! You're it!"

"You're cheating," Beryl giggled as they fell backward onto the leaf pile at the base of the trees. "You can't keep holding onto me, Vale. That's not part of the game."

"Then why are you smiling?" Avalanche asked.

Beryl blushed, swiping at him with her claws. "Stop looking at me like that."

"I can't help where my eyes go. And anyways, Beryl, when are you ever coming to practice diving with me?"

"I'm not confident in the clouds yet."

"You won't get faster if you don't practice."

Beryl looked away, smiling at the forest floor. "All right, Vale. Next time you go up, I'll come with you."

Avalanche held up a claw. "Promise?"

"Aye, I promise."

They traded shy smiles, reading each other's minds. *We should see where the others are. Probably lost.*

Probably getting in trouble.

Avalanche began to stand up, then ducked back down when he heard a Bat shriek deep within the trees. Beryl held her breath. The single high-pitched shriek turned into a mass of dreadful noise, so loud that both young Bats lowered their heads into the leaves.

"What's going on?" Beryl whispered.

"I don't know."

"I should get home."

Shh. Avalanche yanked her back as she tried to crawl away from him. *Something terrible is out there. Dangerous.* The shrieks were getting closer. And there were voices of purebred Elves. *Soldiers.*

Beryl's eyes widened at the sound of a nearby young Bat's wings being torn from his fragile body, and Avalanche inadvertently pressed a claw over her mouth before she could cry out. They shivered under the pile of tree bark scraps, looking into each other's eyes, their hearts racing.

They're killing us, Avalanche said.

Who?

Stay down. Don't breathe.

Who, Vale?

The purebreds.

"Home," Beryl suddenly said out loud, wrestling free from Vale's grasp.

"Beryl, no!"

Avalanche watched her take off running, daring to open her wings and fly through the thick of the forest, weaving around trunks and branches in a graceless pattern.

"Beryl!" He followed, unable to see who or what was ahead of them. Flames and smoke blocked all sense of direction. The entire land was set alight as the shouts of the soldiers grew closer.

Avalanche, help me. Help. Beryl's voice echoed in his mind.

I'm coming, Beryl. Hold on.

He flew beyond the forest into an unfamiliar clearing and tried to see through the smoke swirling about the grass.

"Hold her down! Bring the she-bat alive!"

Beryl.

Avalanche shrieked into the sky and tucked in his wings as he dove blindly toward the soldiers.

"Get off her!" He shrieked again, lungs burning with his rage. "Beryl!"

"Shoot him down!" a soldier yelled. "Shoot that beast down now!"

Dodging arrows in the black sky, Avalanche withdrew a clawful of pyro-cannon from the secret pocket in his tunic and threw it into the mayhem below. He saw the intended flash from the rock's explosion and dropped in a cannonball toward the soldiers. "Beryl!"

"Vale!"

Avalanche saw her looking up at him. She was bound with several ropes and the purebred standing over her seemed both disgusted and smitten by the catch.

"Let Beryl go, soldier," Avalanche called down to him.

"I'm no soldier," the purebred said in a self-assured voice.

Just as Avalanche was about to throw more pyro-cannon, he felt the weight of a massive chain press onto his shoulder blades and wings. He dropped from the sky, vision blurring as he landed hard on the ground.

The purebred Elf stood over him. "I'm Count Deoraheii," he said. "Your Beryl is mine."

Avalanche, struggling to gain balance, watched the blur of soldiers mount their horses. He heard Beryl shrieking for him. *Beryl.* He wanted to scream her name but nothing came out. The weight of the chains on his spine kept him from crawling forward. *Beryl, I'm coming.* Before he could feel her thoughts come back to him, Avalanche blacked out.

<u>Present Day: Vinhdiragh</u>

He stands alone, Avalanche thought as he approached Count Deoraheii on the rooftop. The house was a modest structure, but the land around it blossomed with winter flowers. The beauty of the blooms contrasted against the ugly outline of the count. The one who had taken Beryl. *Beryl.* The she-bat Avalanche had dreamed to pledge his heart to. *My love I shall avenge. I can still hear her cries.*

"Where is she? Where is my beloved?"

"You were a child then, Bat." Deoraheii didn't turn around as he spoke back. He sighed as he took in the chaos around him. "What business did you have with a female?"

"Where is Beryl? Tell me."

"Tell you what?"

Avalanche began to stutter as the memory of Beryl's sweet voice overtook him. "I'd..I'd surrender my...surrender my weapons...surrender anything to be with her again...please...."

"Where has your pride gone, Bat?" Deoraheii still had his back turned.

"She can't be dead. I didn't feel her death the way the others felt it."

"The truth," Deoraheii said, finally facing Avalanche, "will break your heart. And you will die right where you stand."

"Please, count. Tell me."

His words came out in a cruel whisper. "She didn't die that night."

"Then where did she go?" Avalanche strode forward. "What did you do with her?"

The sound of Spindle's calls to his crew rose above the rooftops. Vulkie and Firestorm shrieked as they dove headfirst into clusters of Bloodmanghe on the ground.

"You know what we did to her."

"No...not my Beryl." Avalanche screamed, lunging forward, but failed to draw his blades. He stumbled, falling to his knees, and remained there, body shaking with sobs.

"You Elf Bats let emotion get the best of you." Count Deoraheii grabbed the Bat's twin blades and circled him. "It's no wonder that you rank so low on the list of Elf breeds." He threw the blades off the roof. "No logic, no clear mind, just a pointless stream of rage." Drawing a jagged knife from his cloak, the count knelt behind Avalanche and whispered, "she did die, Bat. She died giving birth to my child."

At Avalanche's tearful gasp, he went on. "I kept Beryl as my pet for a year. The little beast arrived at the start of the next."

Feeling the blade pressed to his throat, Avalanche kept his head down as he let out a shaky breath. "Is the child alive?"

"A daughter. I named her Felsite."

"Is she alive?" Avalanche asked, voice quivering.

"Yes," Deoraheii said, pressing the knife further into Avalanche's throat. "Felsite lives."

SNOWBLIND

"Deoraheii!" Snowblind shouted. His voice cracked as he sprinted across the roof, charging for the count. He speared him with his twin blades, dragging him backward, away from Avalanche.

"Stop!" Avalanche crawled forward, gripping his claws around Snowblind's arm. "He's a father."

"They all are," Snowblind said. "They all pay. Where's your fight, Vale?"

"Beryl's daughter. She had a daughter." Avalanche tried to speak without shivering as he looked at Deoraheii. "He's her father."

Snowblind looked angrily from Avalanche to the count. *My daughters were slaughtered. You dishonored them all. You and your kin, count.* He slashed his blades through the count's neck and flung his body off the roof. Avalanche stared over the edge.

"Avalanche, come. This is our night." Snowblind offered his claw. "Not theirs."

"I can't kill," Avalanche said softly.

"What?"

"I don't want to kill. Felsite. Not Felsite. Beryl's little girl."

"You're in shock." *Brother, you need to come with me.* "We're not harming the women here. We're defending them. Come on. Come!"

"I have to find Felsite, Snow. I have to find her."

"Avalanche!" Snowblind watched him dive erratically off into the fray below. *Your emotions run high. Your mind is weak.* "Avalanche!"

11

Two Kings, One Honor

FLY

"My King Averee." Fly pushed the hood of her cloak back upon entering the citadel's court.

"You have returned to me, child. Have you come to beg forgiveness?" Averee turned from the long table, his bejeweled right hand pushing an empty wine glass aside. He laid his eyes on her.

"We came to kill you," Fly said.

Kiah walked in and stood beside her. Averee looked from one Bat to the other. "You've returned as a Bat," he said.

"Aye," Kiah whispered. "She has."

"You sacrificed physical strength for cunning wile." He lifted a hand and his personal guards descended from the stairs behind him. "Am I right to assume that my cherished book is gone?"

"I burned it to ashes," Fly said. "It was a pleasure to see it disappear."

Averee snarled at her as he stepped forward. "You should not care for their fate."

"I'm their queen."

The guards gripped the hilts of their weapons as Averee reached out a hand to touch Fly's rough-skinned cheek. "Your death will come swiftly, child."

Fly bared her sharp fangs, whipping her head back. "So will yours."

"Neither of you will leave this court with a beating heart."

With her back to the windows, Fly gazed intently at Kiah as she slowly raised her arms. Averee's eyes shifted to Kiah, watching him take a step backward. Fly's snarl transformed into a sly grin as she stared down the king.

"What are you doing, ugly girl?" Averee asked. "Why are you looking at me like that?"

"Siebasacr!" Fly shrieked, her face to the ceiling.

Suddenly the glass shattered around them from the force of a thousand bats flying through the citadel, led by Kiah's bat Siebasacr. Fly continued to hold her arms out in a stance of resolved power. She stood against the fury of the animals as they circled around her, descending onto Averee and his guards.

Well done, my love. Kiah grinned. He rushed forward with Fly, taking out the guards as they were swarmed by bats.

"We are giving you what you want," Kiah said to Averee as he waited for him to get back to his feet.

"What do I want, Bat?" Averee growled. He spat out two broken teeth.

Kiah drew his twin blades. "War."

Spindle, Fly thought. Her eyes were wide as she sensed trouble outside the citadel's walls. *He needs help.*

"Go," Kiah said. *I'll do this alone.*

KIAH

At Fly's exit, he circled Averee, white cloak drifting above the smooth floor. "Why the Death Order? Why my people?"

"Your kind destroyed mine first."

"Oh?" Kiah enjoyed the king's mental torment as he anxiously kept his eyes on the Bat. "How did we?"

"The splintered group. Your great-grandfather led it."

"He did not. He was enslaved by the bloodletters."

"He enjoyed drinking purebred blood."

"You have your history wrong, king. You are as old as he was. You envied us. You wanted our wings and our magic."

"I slayed none."

"You slayed us all."

Averee lifted his greatsword from its place against the wall and lined the blade parallel to Kiah's light twin blades. "My people think I am weak. That I am cursed. I am nothing of the kind, Bat."

Kiah ducked at the first heavy swing, whirling around to his back. Averee turned, crossing his sword against Kiah's left blade. "I have more power in my body and in my sword than you."

"I have speed," Kiah said with a steady breath.

"I am not a sickly king," Averee said. "I reserved my strength for the proper time to use it."

Strength for my family. Strength for my beloved. For Mama. For Father. Kiah drew in power from the memories of childhood, the fading image of Mama kneeling with a blade at her neck. "You violated all of our females."

Averee grinned at Kiah's snarl. "When my soldiers finish off your wife, you will have nothing left to fight for."

Butterfly. Kiah spun, slamming his body into Averee with open wings. *My love, what is that shiver in your body? What is that look in your eyes?* He thought of Fly's voice, the way in which her mind was turning. *What are you not telling me?*

"Your people will be ripped apart by my soldiers, Bat. Every last one of your brethren will shriek as they are dissected alive."

"They will survive this night," Kiah growled. He backflipped across the court, crouching before his charge against Averee. "All of them."

"Accept your fate, Bat."

They clashed blades.

"You will not live to see the sunrise!"

"I fight in Jekkiliah's stead, Averee. He taught me what a true king does for his people."

"Your father was an animal the same as you. There are no royal Elf Bats."

No! Kiah whirled, striking the edge of Averee's sword. "I am king. More of a king than you."

"There is no honor among beasts of the dark. You crawl through filthy caves, fly with black dragon wings. Crooked fangs, wretched claws. You are nothing."

I will carry this line with my Butterfly. We will bear children to continue the Bat legacy. That is my duty. Our duty to this world.

"Look at the distance in your eyes, Bat. Your distracted mind is my gain."

"You will not take my Butterfly," Kiah said. "Nor will you sacrifice my brethren."

Averee backed up to the stairs, sword raised. "I am not the only enemy of your people. You will always be hunted."

Kiah flew over him, landing further up the stairs. He crossed his blades at his chest. "This is my game, Averee. Not yours."

"The game you're playing is over." Averee swung his sword down hard, breaking Kiah's right blade in half.

This strength is not possible. Fly said he was weak. How does he fight with such vigor?

"I've kept this a secret, Hezekiah," Averee said, following him up the stairs. "My kin does not know what I can do to any of them. The Bloodmanghe may defend my court, but I take care of myself. I didn't just order the Elf Bat massacre. I took part in it."

Kiah used the hilt of his remaining blade as a block, spinning away from Averee's sword. They dueled up each flight of stairs, spiraling toward the citadel's roof.

12

Bloodmanghe

FLY

Fly ran toward Spindle where he shouted orders at his crew. "I need a diversion! They're using the children as shields!"

The Bloodmanghe had taken over the city. Elflings and their parents were caught in the crossfire, wounded in their attempts to defend themselves from the burly soldiers.

"Fly, distract the soldiers!" Spindle yelled.

One of the Bloodmanghe picked up an elfling girl, holding her by the throat. Fly drew her blade and stared the soldier down. "Free the child," Fly said. "Free her!" *I once roamed these streets as a little girl. I was once like her. Give the children up, Bloodmanghe.*

"Fly, arrows!" Ty screamed as he dropped from the sky. Fly turned her head to see Tor about to fire a trio of arrows from the rooftop. She ducked and sprinted to the right, finding herself standing back-to-back with Vulkie.

"With me," Vulkie said to her, whirling his blades above his head. "The Bloodmanghe."

Fly charged hard against the Bloodmanghe with Vulkie. The soldier dropped the elfling to fight them back.

Take him down, Vulkie, Fly said. *I'll help the girl.*

"Come, little one." Fly dropped to one knee and held out a claw. "I'll help you find your mother."

The girl crawled backward, whimpering as Fly tried to approach her. "It's okay," Fly said. "I'm not going to hurt you."

"Bloodmanghe! Bloodmanghe from the citadel!" Spindle called out. "The king's guard is emptying! Deflect them, Bats!"

The amber glow of torches lit up the blood-stained ground around her as Fly crawled toward the elfling girl. "I'll protect you, little one," she said.

"Bloodletter," the girl whispered.

"No. Not a bloodletter. I'm a friend."

"Butterfly, run!" Tor shrieked from the roof. "Bloodmanghe!"

Looking over her shoulder, Fly saw a pack of the soldiers armed with gritty crossbows and axes steering toward her and the girl.

All right. Fear me or not, she thought, *I'm getting us out of here.* She dove forward, aiming to grab the girl in her arms, but the little elfling sprinted away down the main road of Adreachterum. "I'm trying to help you!" Fly shouted. She opened her wings and flew between the houses. Children scattered before her, terrified of the shadow that chased them.

SPINDLE

"Kill the she-bat! Bring her down!" a Bloodmanghe called out.

Spindle saw the lot of them switch direction and climb up the rooftops to run after Fly. Their crossbows were trained on her as she flew low.

"Protect our queen!" Vulkie desperately screamed as he dueled a pair of Bloodmanghe on his own. "She carries the heir!"

*Heir...Fly carries a baby Bat...Kiah's baby...*Spindle looked to the stretch of houses swarmed by the soldiers. Fly was their target. She carried the last Elf Bat heir.

Butterfly...oh no...

"Typhoon, Tornado, follow me!" Spindle shouted as he ran down the road.

FLY

Fly called out to the children beneath her, desperate for them to turn around. Her frantic cries changed to wordless screeching as she watched them run for their lives. They ran from her straight into the Bloodmanghe and so did she, wings ensnared in an impromptu trap.

"Kill the she-bat!" the Bloodmanghe growled. "Tear the wings from her back!"

Spindle, where are you? Fly extended her claws as far as she could, tearing through the netting encasing her. She shrieked as the Bloodmanghe surrounded her, the streaks of color in her eyes flashing bright in rhythm with her rapid heartbeat. "Get away from me!" She tried to grab the blades at her back.

"Butterfly!" Ty and Tor had their bows raised together, firing arrow after arrow into the circle of Bloodmanghe. "Crawl out, love," they said to her. "Come!"

Spindle pulled Butterfly out from beneath the net, his own cutlass stained with fresh blood as he whirled to face an oncoming Bloodmanghe. "Fight, girl," he said. "Stay close to me."

"Aye, Spindle," Fly said breathlessly. She looked up toward the citadel as the dark of the night gave way to the deep blue of early morning light. She saw two figures facing each other on the citadel's roof. Kiah and Averee. *He needs to know*, she thought. *He needs to know about our son.*

13

Ixetmori's Army

KIAH

"You're gentler than I thought you would be," Averee said. "Not as fierce as your ancestors."

"I do not wish to kill."

"But you will. You see me as a sacrifice the same as I saw your kin."

"Elf Bats are worth protecting, Averee."

"You have the advantage, Bat. Leap off. Fly away. Show your true loyalty to your brothers," Averee taunted. "Show them you're afraid."

Kiah tightened his claw around his blade. "Averee, purebred snake, you cannot live to pass a second death order."

"My liege!" A wide-eyed messenger Elf came between the two, grabbing hold of Averee's wrist as he looked him in the eye.

"Spawn of goblin blood, guard! What allows you to interrupt this?"

The young purebred was shaking as he pointed toward the stretch of meadow. "Ixetmori comes."

Averee followed his gaze. Kiah gave a snarl before looking out with him. *Humans. What are they doing here?*

"She does not come as a friend, my liege," the messenger said.

"And how do you know that?" Averee growled at him.

They watched as three guards of the king rode out to intercept the human army. All three were shot dead by Ixetmori's front line archers within minutes of exiting Adreachterum's gate.

"My liege, what are your orders? Do we retaliate?"

Averee was speechless.

"They're not advancing. We have time," the nervous messenger said. "My king Averee, I've seen how humans attack. They're going to fire relentlessly upon our city and then charge in when only the weak remain. Ixetmori will take everything."

Nine hundred, Kiah counted of the army. *No peace in their eyes. Ixetmori...the woman who abandoned Fly. Does she come for the Bats?*

"Ruthless, callous, barbaric..." Averee whispered to himself, blade slipping from his hand. "Why must you turn against me, lady of wiles?"

The purebred king fears her. The humans must be a greater enemy than us, Kiah thought.

Fly flew overhead, landing on the roof next to Kiah. "Did you summon her, Averee?"

"I called no one," Averee said. He looked out at the meadow with an anxious sigh. "Your father was right about the letters, child. Ixetmori has come to wipe out the city."

"And you wish us to defend you, my liege, after what you have done to us?"

Averee looked into Fly's angry eyes. "You Bats claim you would not let an innocent soul perish without a fight. If not for my life, Butterfly, daughter of Addis, please defend our children."

"We have no reason to stay," Fly said. "The night is over." She looked to Kiah. *Let's go home, love.*

Wait for me, Kiah said. He turned to Averee as Fly took off, disappearing into the city. "She is right, Averee. What reason do we have to remain in the carnage?"

Averee stepped close, spitting words in his face. "Your Bat brethren and pirate allies have weakened my defenses. My soldiers will not outlast that army. Say you stand with us, Hezekiah."

"Why should we do anything to protect your people?"

"Ixetmori won't end her wrath here. She will hunt you down one at a time, Bat. I know you know nothing of Fly's history with that woman, but I say to you, Ixetmori is deadly for all Elves. She will slaughter the very children that your wife tried to protect!"

Kiah thought silently as the purebred king stood trembling.

"You wretched beasts owe us your blades. All of you!" Averee screamed.

For the children. We have to save the children, Fly. "You have my word, Averee," Kiah whispered. "For the children." He shoved him toward the edge of the roof as he spread his wings. "You stay out of our way."

FLY

"Come, Spindle," Kiah said from the air. "Reposition for arrow rain. Attack on my order." He saw Snowblind collecting arrows and Vulkie eagerly packing pyro-cannon into his ammo sling. "Spread your remaining crew out to the villages. On my order, Spindle," he repeated.

"Aye, Bat."

"Get everyone inside! Ty, Fire, take the west perimeter! Watch their movement."

Come with me, pudding, Kiah said. *The barn.* He landed, taking Fly's claw in his and running with her to the southernmost part of Adreachterum. An empty barn for their shelter.

"Kiah," Fly started to say. "Kiah, I need to tell you—"

"Stay here, love," Kiah said. "When I lead the attack, you stay."

"But Kiah—"

"Fire arrows!" Spindle yelled. "They're aiming high! Give us the order, Bat!"

Kiah peered around the corner of the outer barn door. A volley of flames lit up the city. He drew back further into the barn, pulling Fly with him. "Wait here with me, love. I'll call the attack soon."

"Kiah, please...don't go out there."

What's wrong, beloved? He looked down into her eyes. "What is it?"

"I don't want you to leave me." Fly fought tears back as he embraced her. "Don't leave me and your son."

KIAH

"What?"

"We're having a baby, Kiah."

The barn's roof crackled and shifted from the flames surrounding it. Kiah stepped back, reaching to touch Fly's cheek wet with tears. "A son?"

"I'm carrying the Bat heir."

"My Butterfly..." His breath shook. "I felt something different in you, pudding. I couldn't imagine that it was..."

"You're going to be a father," Fly said. "We're going to be parents." She started to smile. "Fly away with me. Let's go home."

Ixetmori. The human possessed by demons. She means to kill the Bats. She means to kill our unborn child. Kiah stepped back. "We can't." He slowly shook his head, a sudden wave of grief bringing a sob to his mouth. "It's not finished."

"Let's go home, Kiah. We can fly back now."

"Butterfly, my beloved she-bat...it's too late to walk away."

"Why?" Fly raised her voice as tears streamed down her face. "Why can't we leave?"

*Listen...*Kiah dropped to one knee, taking her claws in his as she knelt with him. "I must go to Ixetmori. I must surrender."

"No. No, you can't. We'll raise our son far from here. We can flee this fight, Kiah!"

"They will run us down, Fly. I have to go to them."

"She'll kill you."

"This is a king's duty," Kiah said. He combed Fly's hair back with his claws and breathed in her scent. "I must protect my family," he whispered, laying a claw on her belly. "Tell him about us."

"No, Kiah," Fly sobbed. "You can't go."

"Give me the order, Bat!" Spindle yelled from outside the barn. "They're moving to burn the villages!

"I have to go, pudding," Kiah said. His voice trembled. "The army will wipe out the city, the villages, they will find us and kill you and our baby. Ixetmori demands a sacrifice. I am that sacrifice."

"No," Fly said. "She wants me. She wants me, Kiah."

The barn was engulfed in flames as Kiah stood, rocking Fly against his chest. "No matter what happens, Fly, tell them to stand down."

"What?"

Ilumiaoacht. He pressed his forehead to hers. *Tell them to stand down.* "Do not follow me."

SPINDLE

"Stand down!" Fly shrieked. She ran past Spindle, waving her arms to the sky. "Don't attack!" Her call was tearful and hoarse. Averee's Bloodmanghe were firing their own arrows onto the human army, refusing to take orders from a she-bat.

Where's she going? Spindle thought. *Where's Kiah?*

"Stand down!" Fly shrieked louder.

Then Spindle saw Kiah. He was walking slowly down the main road, an unwavering determination in his eyes.

"Kiah!" Spindle called out.

Kiah's focus was on something outside the city. Spindle lowered his sword. *The human army. He's attacking alone.*

"Fly, what's he doing?"

"Kiah says to stand down. Don't fight them!"

Spindle climbed onto the top of the wall where Fly was perched. The leader of the army looked ready to obliterate them all. Ixetmori.

Have you lost your mind, Bat?

KIAH

Embers rained down on Kiah as he calmly moved through the road. He felt the heat of the fire and breathed out softly. *Father died protecting Mama and me. He was afraid but he did not let it show. I will do the same.*

"Hezekiah!"

Spindle.

"Kiah, what are you doing? Come back!"

My wild pirate friend, Kiah thought. *I'm going to miss you.* He continued forward, noting the shift in the human army's stance. Suddenly all their arrows were directed at him.

*Kiah...*Fly said.

It's okay, love. Kiah did not falter. He kept his eyes forward.

"No, Fly!" Vulkie screamed.

Keep her safe, brother. Keep my Butterfly safe.

"Fire on the Bat king!" Ixetmori ordered from the meadow. Her harsh voice grated on the ears, matching her rough exterior.

The woman who adopted Fly as her own daughter but who abandoned her without a care. The woman who Snowblind says carries demons. Is it true?

Fly's voice was fading. All voices, all noise and chaos faded around him until he found himself locking eyes with Ixetmori.

"Ixetmori!" Kiah called out. He deflected an incoming arrow with his remaining blade, then let the blade drop to the ground. "I surrender to you."

For my family.

"There is nothing for you to take except me." He walked on, removing his armor piece by piece as he spoke out to Ixetmori. "I am Hezekiah, son of Jekkiliah, grandson of Andricherai, king of the Elf Bats. I give myself to you, Ixetmori, as a sacrifice."

He released the clasp of his cloak, letting it slip off his shoulders onto the grass. Arrows soared around him, the human soldiers firing on the city.

I do this for my kin. "Take me in their place." *The sun rises. Night is over.* "Accept my surrender, leader of Herradhtadya." Kiah stopped walking and raised his arms, wings unfurled at his back. He wore nothing but a thin tunic, leggings, and soft leather boots. The fragility of his Bat body changed the look in Ixetmori's eyes. A smug reverence replaced her vehement glare. *I am not afraid. Take me.*

"Cease fire!" Ixetmori shouted. She waited until her archers had lowered their bows before dismounting her horse. She took three broad steps to stand before Kiah, tilting her head back to look into his bright eyes. "You. You think I would take you as payment for the entire city of Adreachterum?"

"I suffer for my family," Kiah said to her. "You wish to lessen your own anguish at the cost of Elf people. I know this, Ixetmori. You will own me for the rest of my life."

"And," Ixetmori said, "what is the trick? What do you gain by losing your freedom to me?"

Kiah threw a glance over his shoulder and pointed a claw at the city. "My family lives."

"My own Bat to do with as I please." She nodded with an arrogant grin, motioning for two of her soldiers to join them. "Your sacrifice is accepted, Hezekiah."

FLY

Ixetmori placed a metal collar around Kiah's neck and chains on his wings before Fly and the Bat brethren met them in the meadow. Spindle stood farther back. His fingers twitched at his sides as he fought not to strike out at Ixetmori. He lowered his head, refusing to look at any of the Bats.

"Kiah," Fly said quietly. She reached her arms around Kiah, holding him tight. He still smelled like teak wood and cedar. *I love you.*

We will hear each other, my love, Kiah said. *I will hear our little one's thoughts.* He gently kissed Fly. *Ilumiaoacht.*

Fly watched his eyes shift to the eight Bats behind her and she heard him say in a soft voice, "Aonismunidh." A Bat word unfamiliar to her. She waited to hear the thoughts of the others but their minds were silent.

"One day you will know, Fly," Kiah whispered to her. "You will know the meaning."

Don't leave us. Please, Kiah...you don't have to do this.

"Elf Bat, come!" Ixetmori yelled out. She yanked on the chain attached to Kiah's collar, dragging him hard to the ground. "Time to go to your cage."

Kiah... Fly felt Spindle lift her off the ground, holding her back from running after him.

"Kiah!"

She had fought with the strength of Ilumiaoacht, but at the last chilling glance given by Ixetmori, Fly's wings shuddered with a new wave of emotion. The night of revenge had ended for all but one. Ilumiaoacht was gone. The spirit of Vinhdiragh had awoken within her.

About the Author

Han M Greenbarg has been in love with writing fiction since childhood. She is an avid coffee drinker, proud dog mom, and lover of country music and war movies. Her biggest jolts of inspiration stem from nature, a variety of film scores, and animals of all kinds.

You can connect with me on:

https://www.hanmgreenbarg.com

Also by Han M Greenbarg

Elf Bat Book One: Kiah

Twelve years after the ruthless massacre of his parents and most of his kin, eighteen-year-old Elf Bat Kiah lives a life of internalized grief and solitude in his family's cave. The arrival of Fly, a reckless purebred Elf maiden, sparks the flame for revenge and a resurgence of the Bats.

Scurts Flightplan

With three months left to live in a stifling, post-nuclear city, Damon Scurto believes he has one last shot at finding the grave of the woman who got away. He is best friends with a guy who eats paper, best frenemies with a convicted killer, and is the bane of his wine-drunk therapist's existence.